W9-CMO-771

WITHDRAWN

SEP 1 2 2024

NAFC PUBLIC LIBRARY

NEW ALBANY-FLOYD COUNTY PUBLIC LIBRARY
MAY 2 2 2001
YP HE
Heller, Nicholas.
Elwood and the witch /
AV   278322

NEW ALBANY-FLOYD COUNTY LIBRARY

3 3110 00451 6942

Elwood
and the Witch

By **NICHOLAS HELLER**

Pictures by **JOS. A. SMITH**

Greenwillow Books

An Imprint of HarperCollinsPublishers

Gouache, watercolor paints, and watercolor pencils
were used for the full-color art.
The text type is Catull Bold.

Elwood and the Witch
Text copyright © 2000 by Nicholas Heller
Illustrations copyright © 2000 by Jos. A. Smith
All rights reserved. Printed in Singapore by Tien Wah Press.
www.harperchildrens.com

Library of Congress Cataloging-in-Publication Data

Elwood and the Witch/ by Nicholas Heller ;
pictures by Jos. A. Smith.
p.   cm.
"Greenwillow Books."
Summary: While being taken for a wild ride on a witch's
broom and with its angry owner sending spells
skyward, Elwood the pig doesn't know how to land.
ISBN 0-688-16945-7 (trade).   ISBN 0-688-16946-5 (lib. bdg.)
[1. Pigs–Fiction. 2. Witches–Fiction.
3. Brooms and brushes–Fiction.]
I. Smith, Joseph A. (Joseph Anthony), (date) ill. II. Title.
PZ7.H37426 El 2000 [E]-dc21 99-052628

1 2 3 4 5 6 7 8 9 10   First Edition

For young Miles Tierney
—N. H.

This one's for Nick Heller.
Go, Nick, go!
—J. A. S.

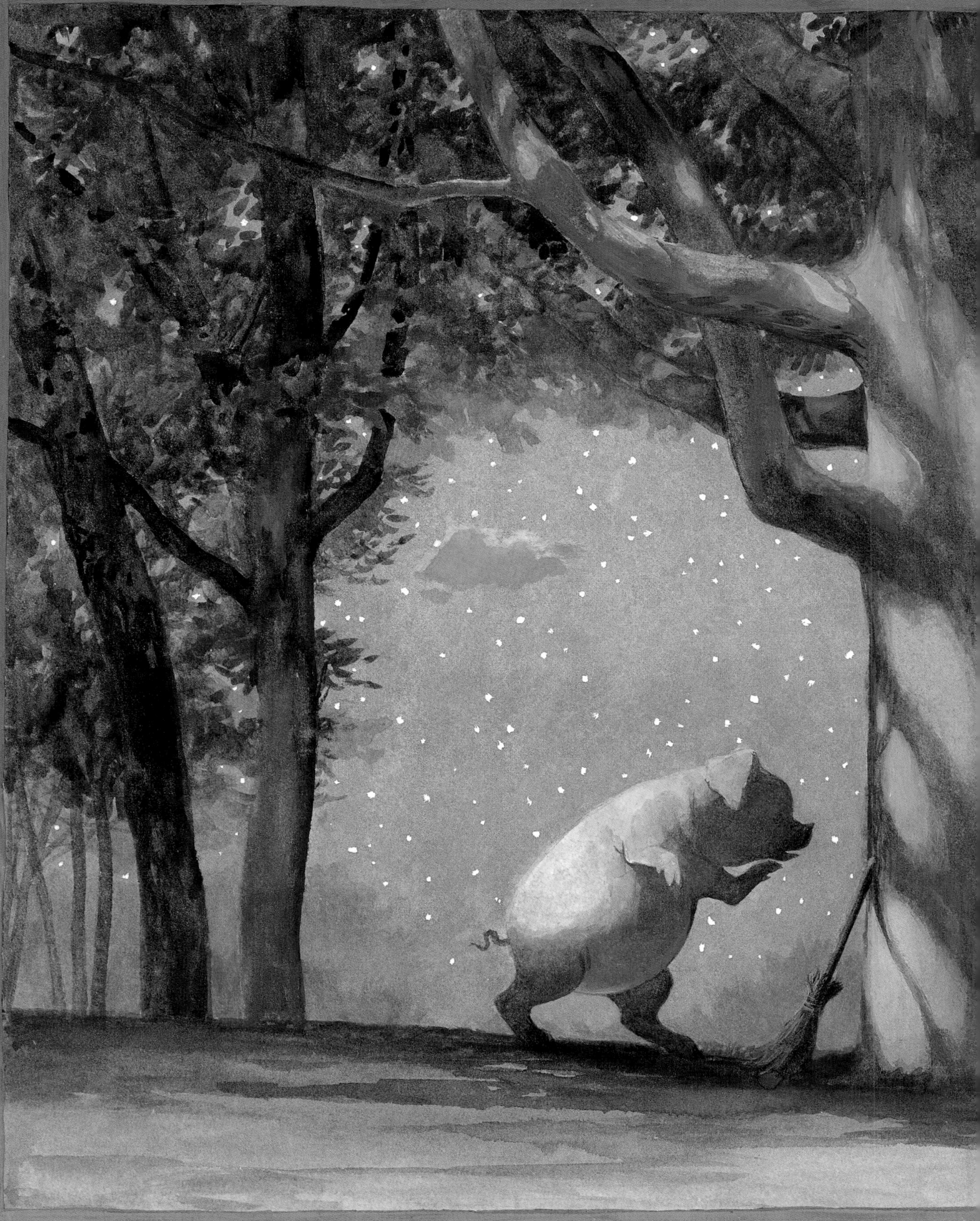

One moonlit evening Elwood found an old broom leaning against the trunk of an oak tree. This will do nicely to keep my front step swept, he thought happily.

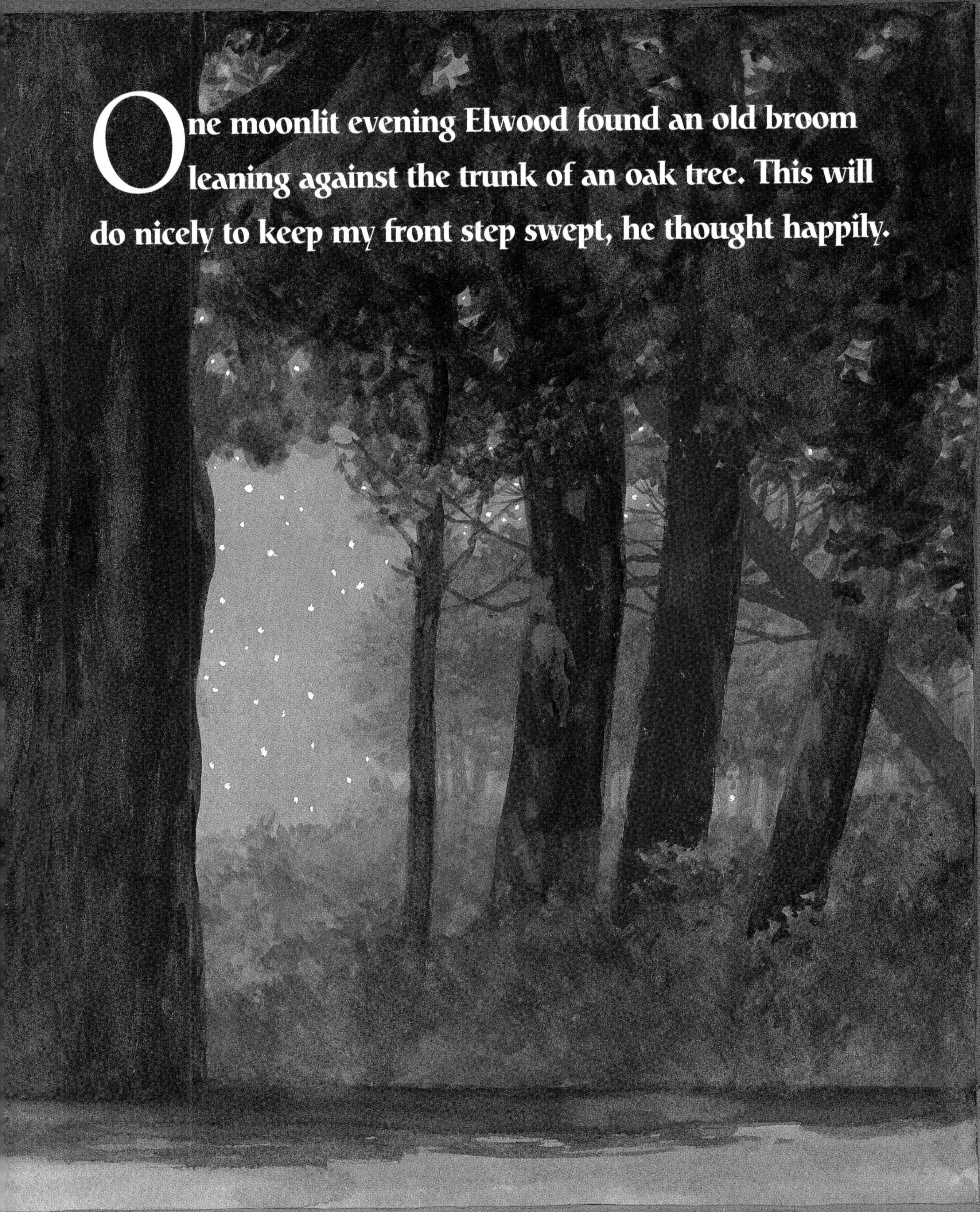

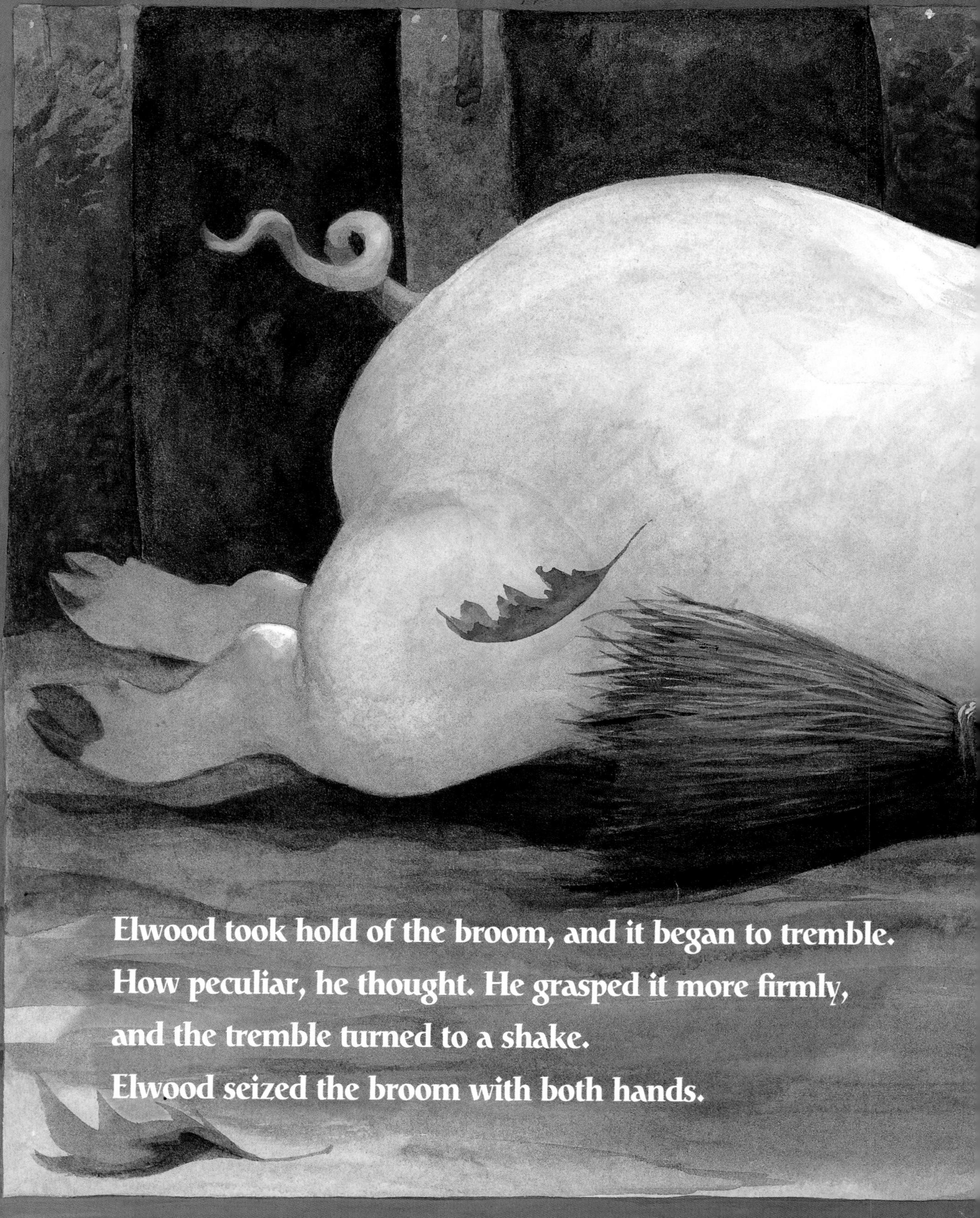

Elwood took hold of the broom, and it began to tremble.
How peculiar, he thought. He grasped it more firmly,
and the tremble turned to a shake.
Elwood seized the broom with both hands.

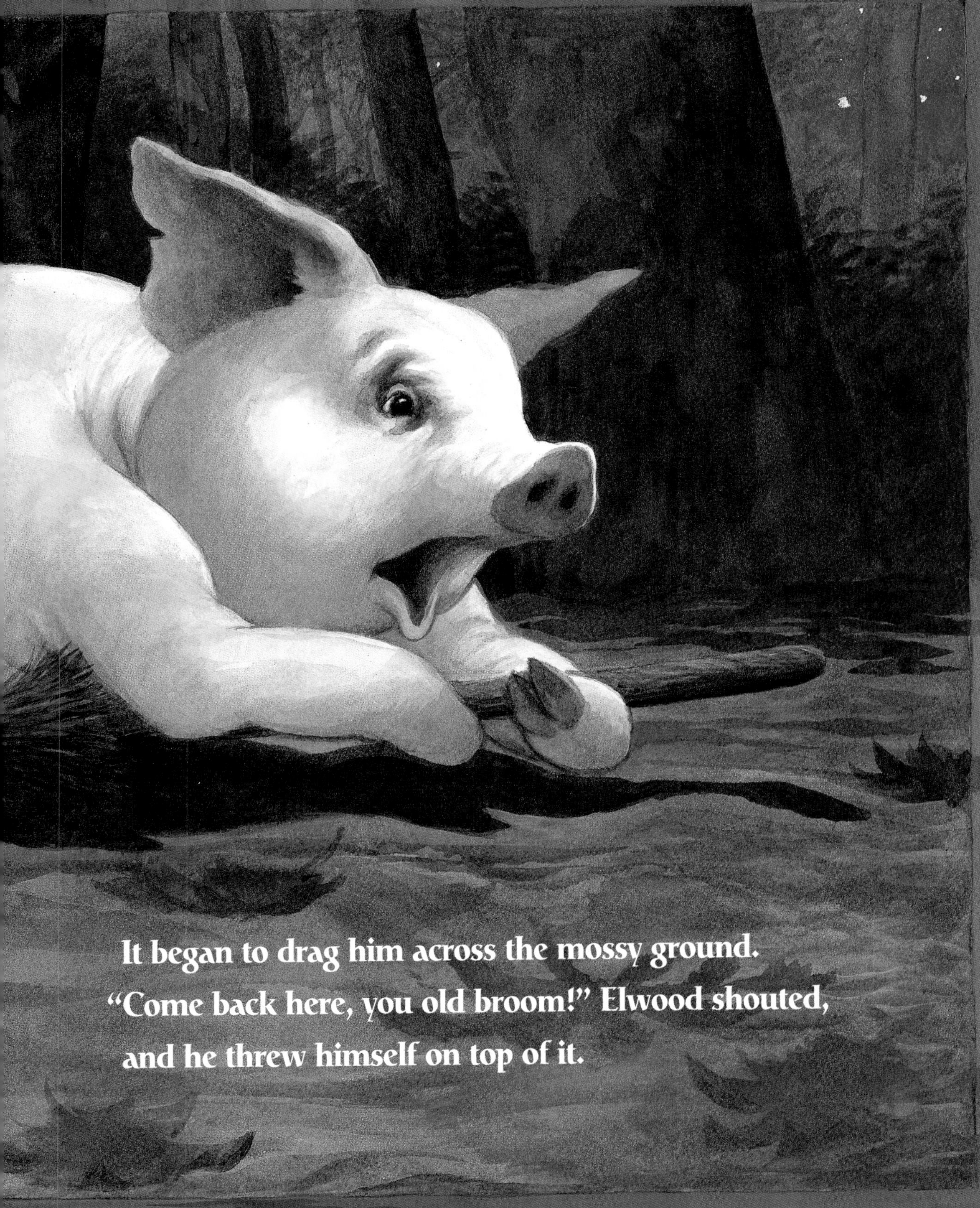

It began to drag him across the mossy ground.
"Come back here, you old broom!" Elwood shouted,
and he threw himself on top of it.

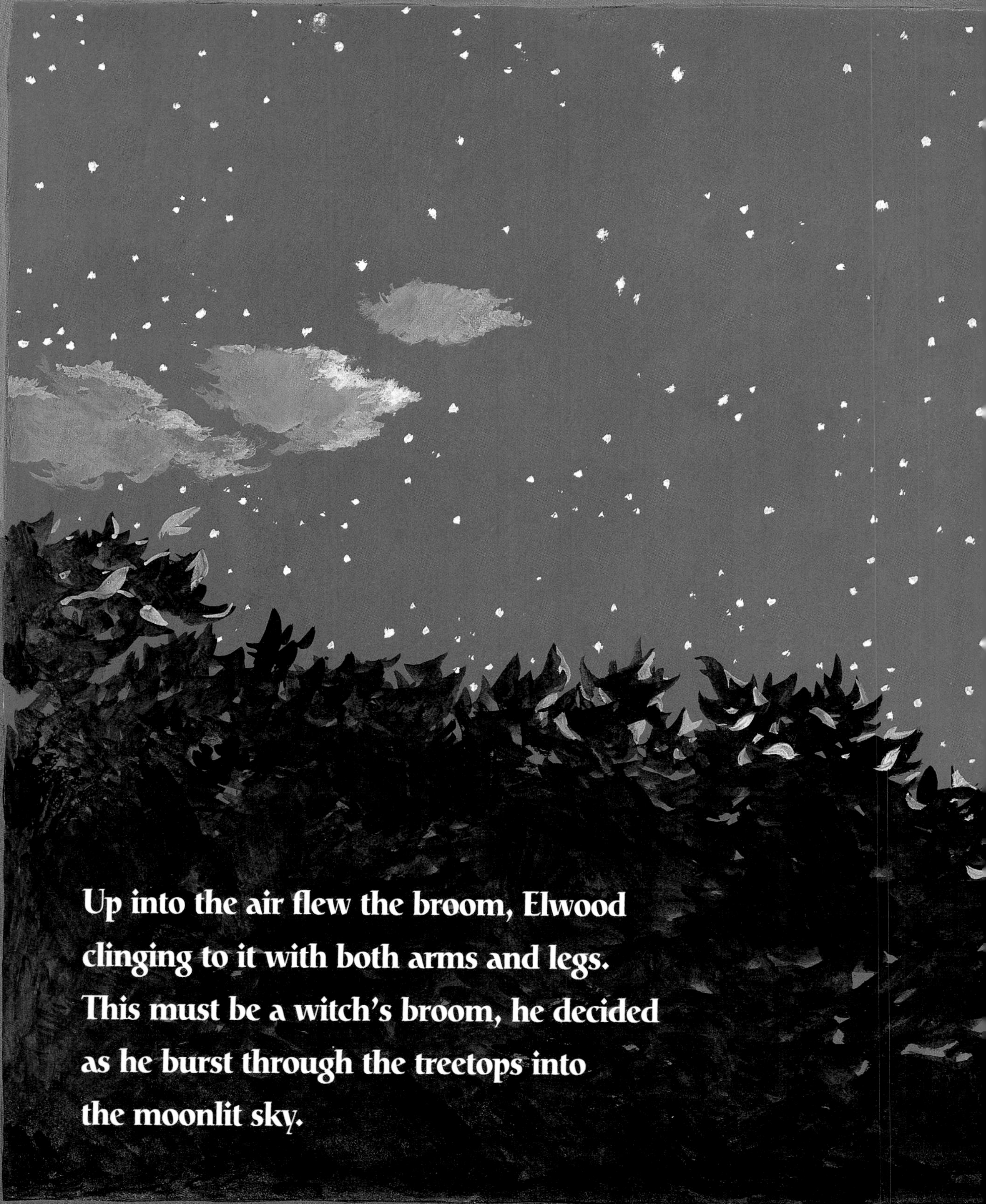

Up into the air flew the broom, Elwood clinging to it with both arms and legs. This must be a witch's broom, he decided as he burst through the treetops into the moonlit sky.

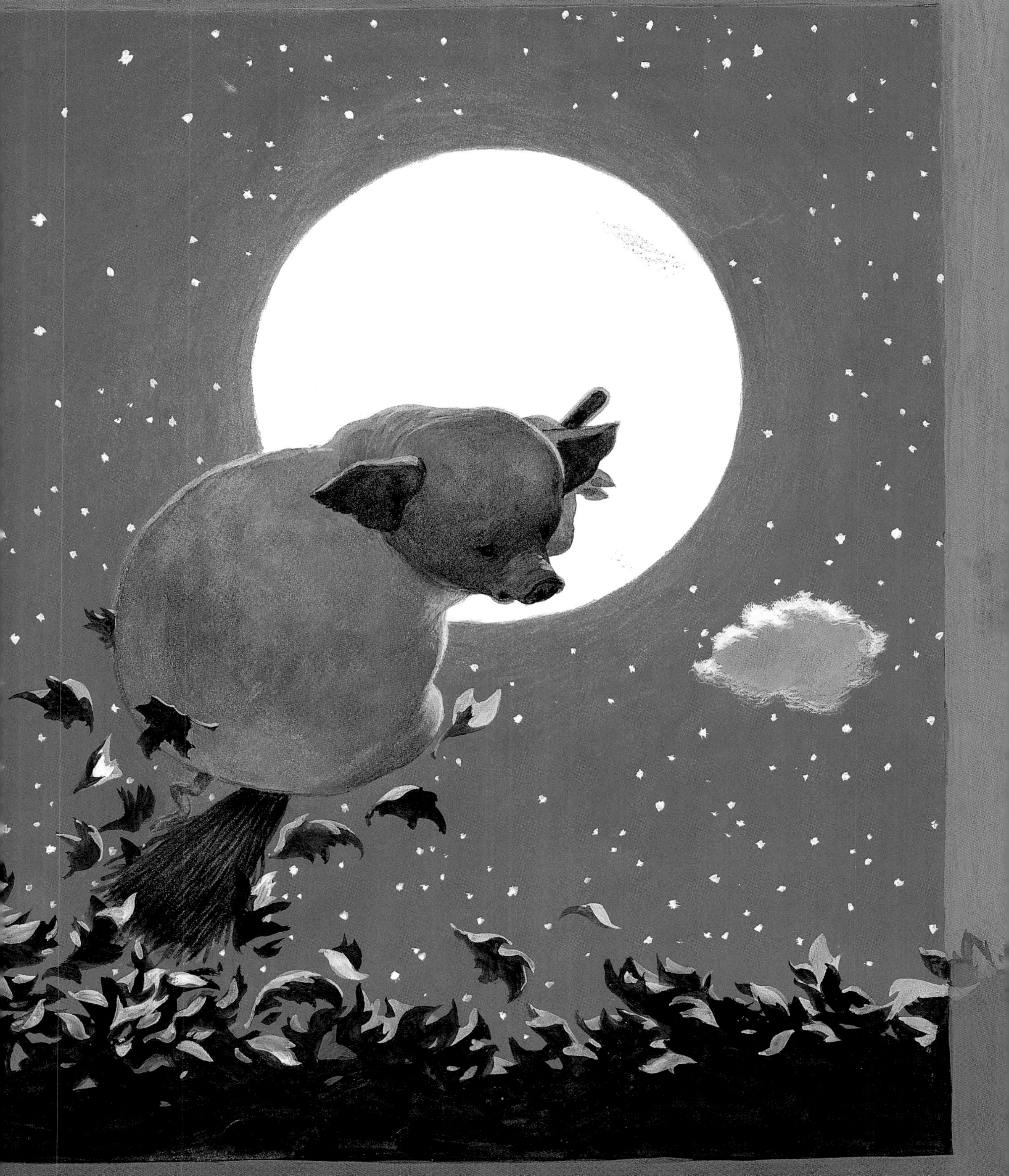

Just then Elwood heard a bloodcurdling screech.
He looked down to see a witch come charging
out from under the trees, waving her fists.
She had been in the woods collecting bitter
roots and poisonous toadstools when she saw
Elwood go sailing past.
"Thief!" she screamed. "Come back here
with my broom!"

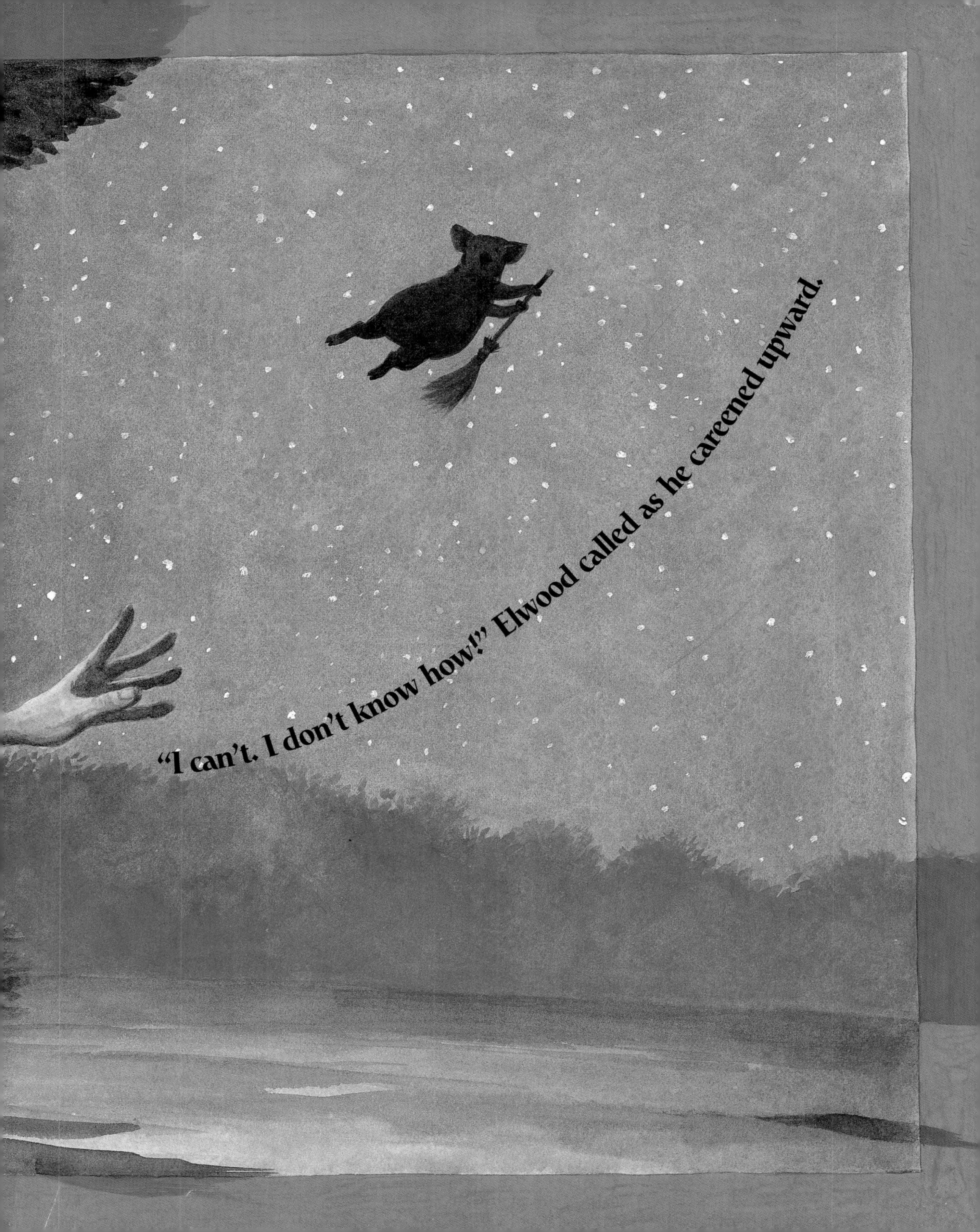

"I can't. I don't know how!" Elwood called as he careened upward.

The witch was too angry to listen.
"Come back here," she cried, "or I'll turn you into a . . . a . . . a . . . a trout!"
The witch raised her arms and shot off a spell.
Elwood felt the tip of his tail tingle as the spell whizzed by, inches away.

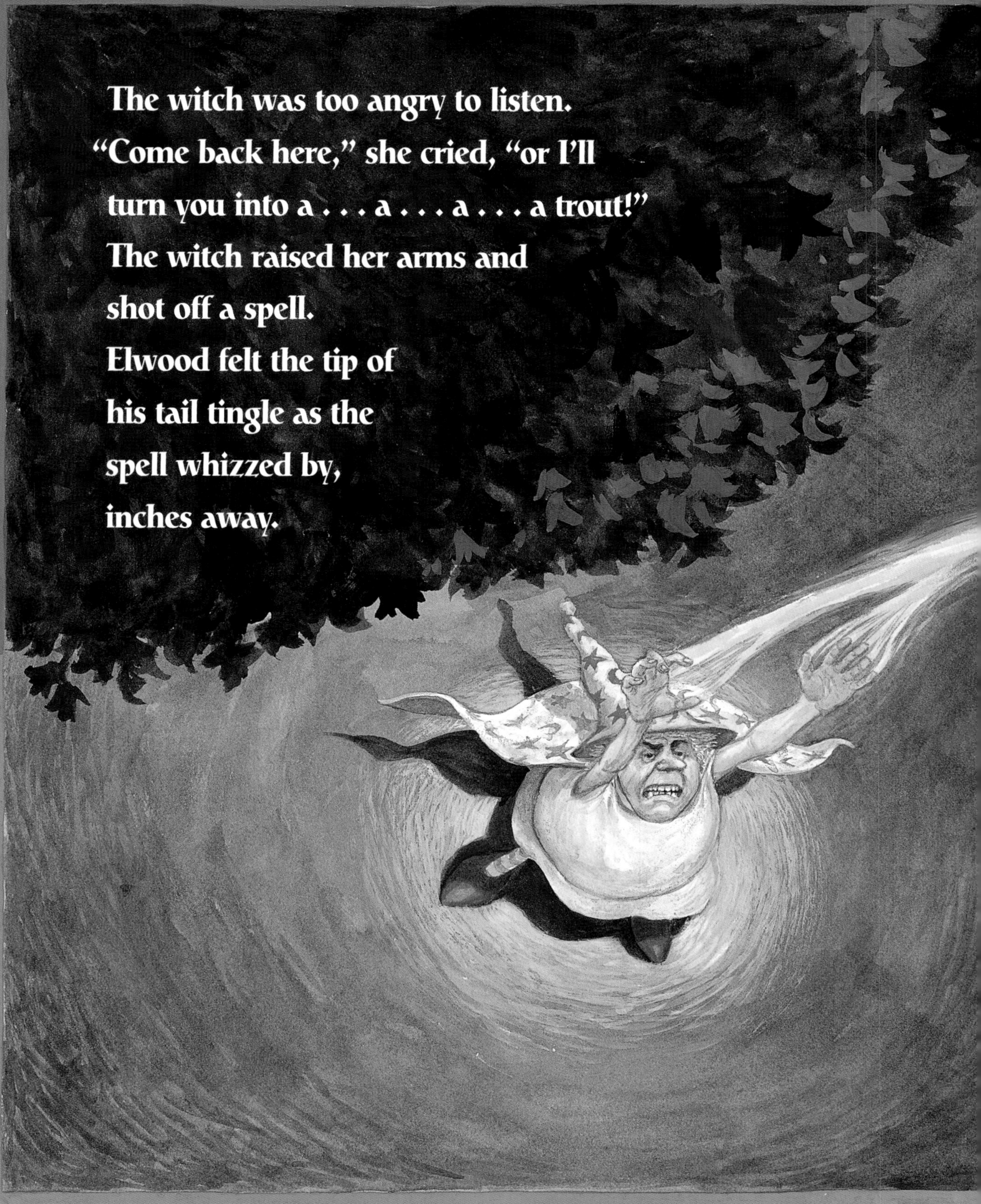

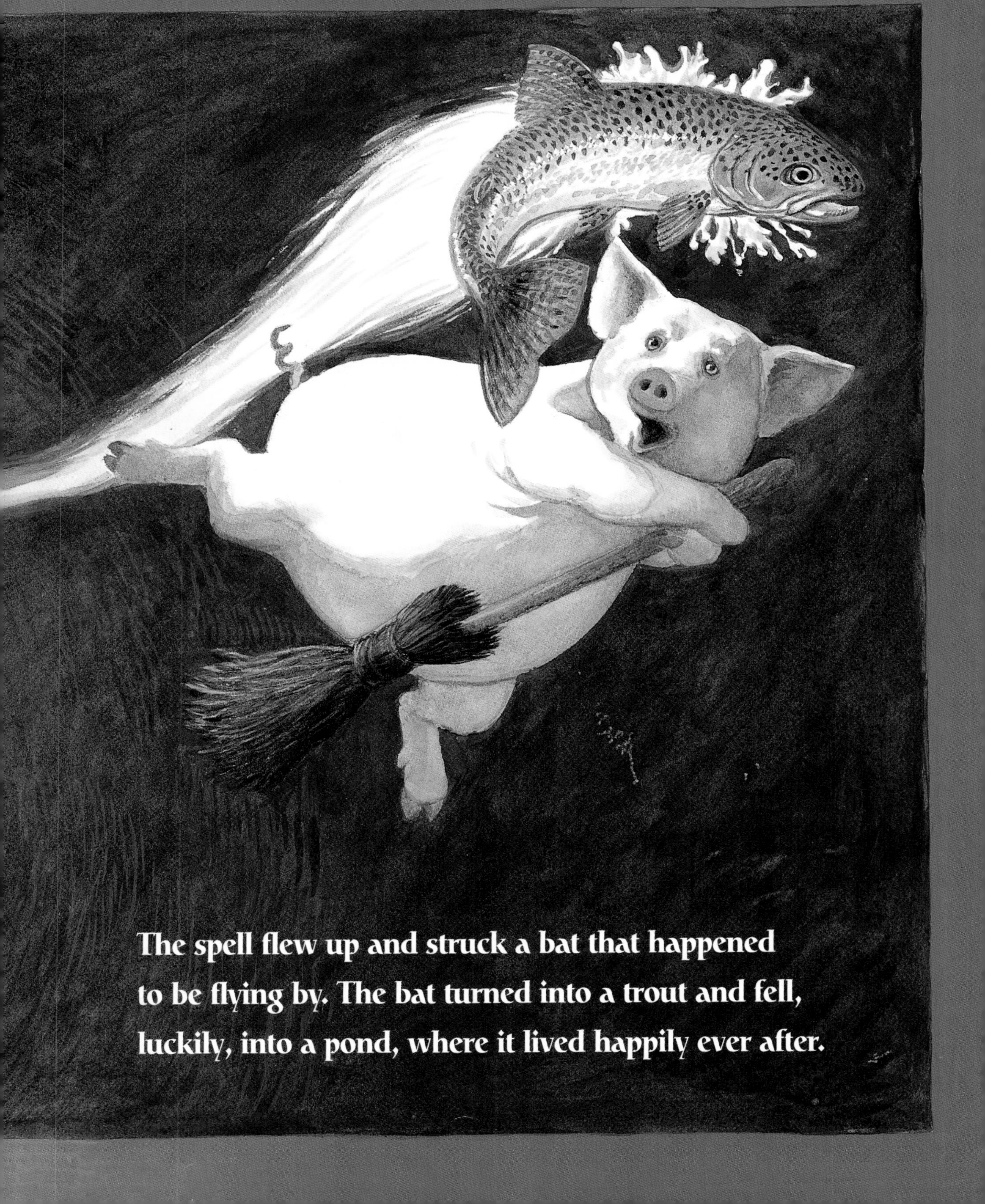

The spell flew up and struck a bat that happened to be flying by. The bat turned into a trout and fell, luckily, into a pond, where it lived happily ever after.

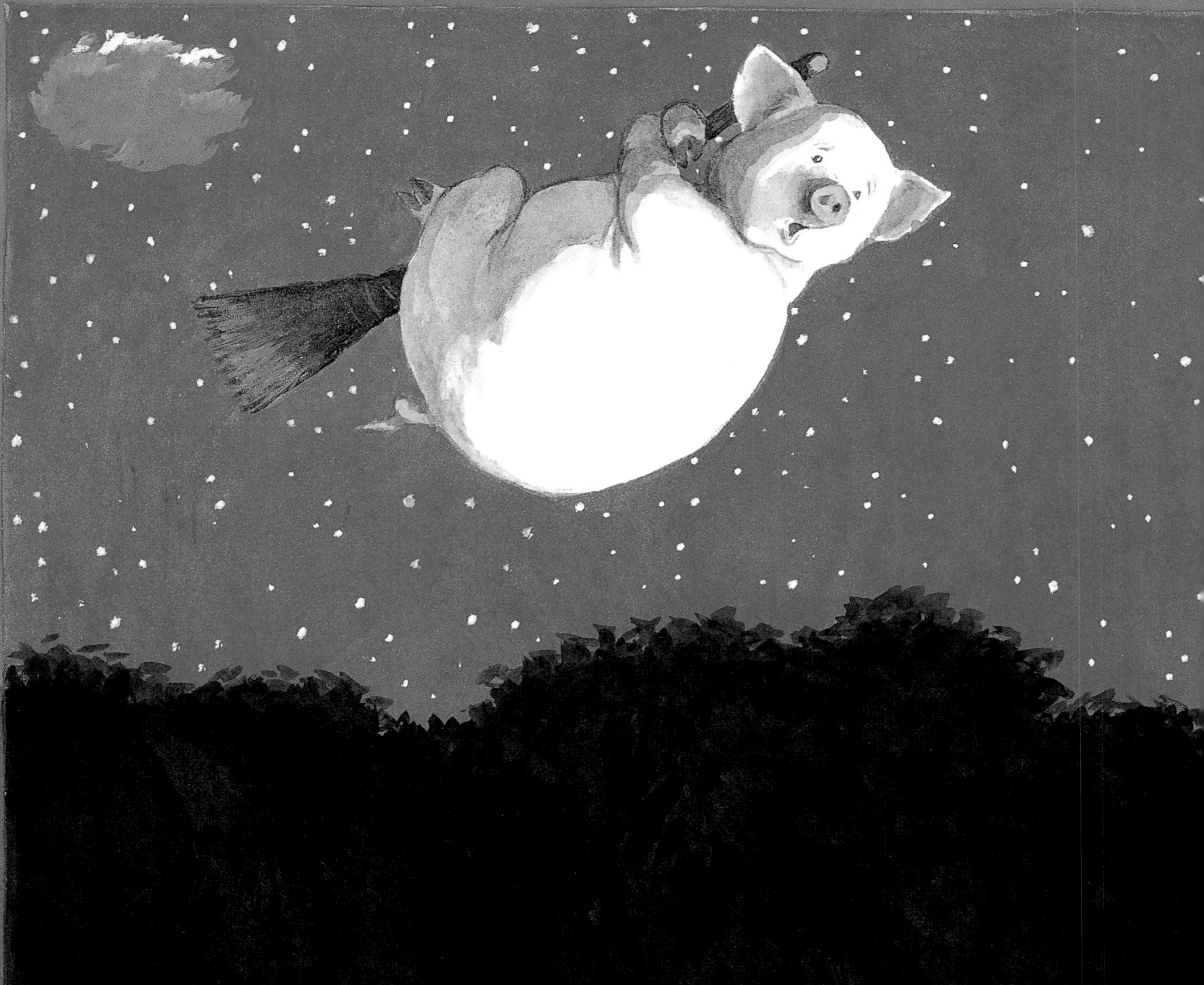

"Drat!" screeched the witch furiously. "Bring me back my broom, or I'll turn you into a . . . a . . . a . . . a toad!"

"I don't know how!" wailed Elwood again as the broom swooped overhead.

The witch didn't listen.

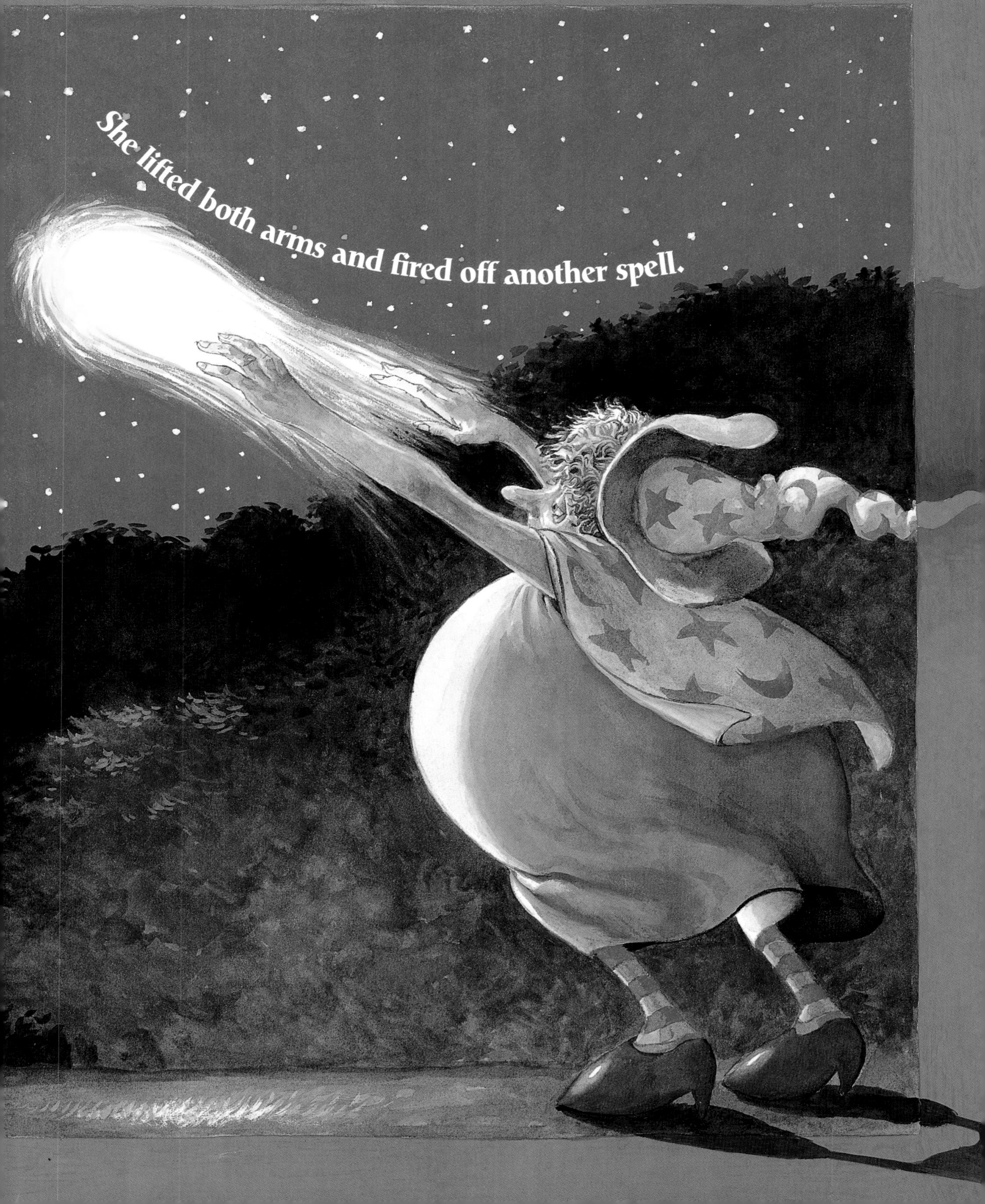

She lifted both arms and fired off another spell.

Elwood felt his snout tingle as the spell passed just in front of him. The spell rocketed up and hit a passing cloud.

The cloud turned into a giant toad. It looked about, somewhat puzzled, then kicked its big back legs and swam off through the sky, where it can still sometimes be seen.

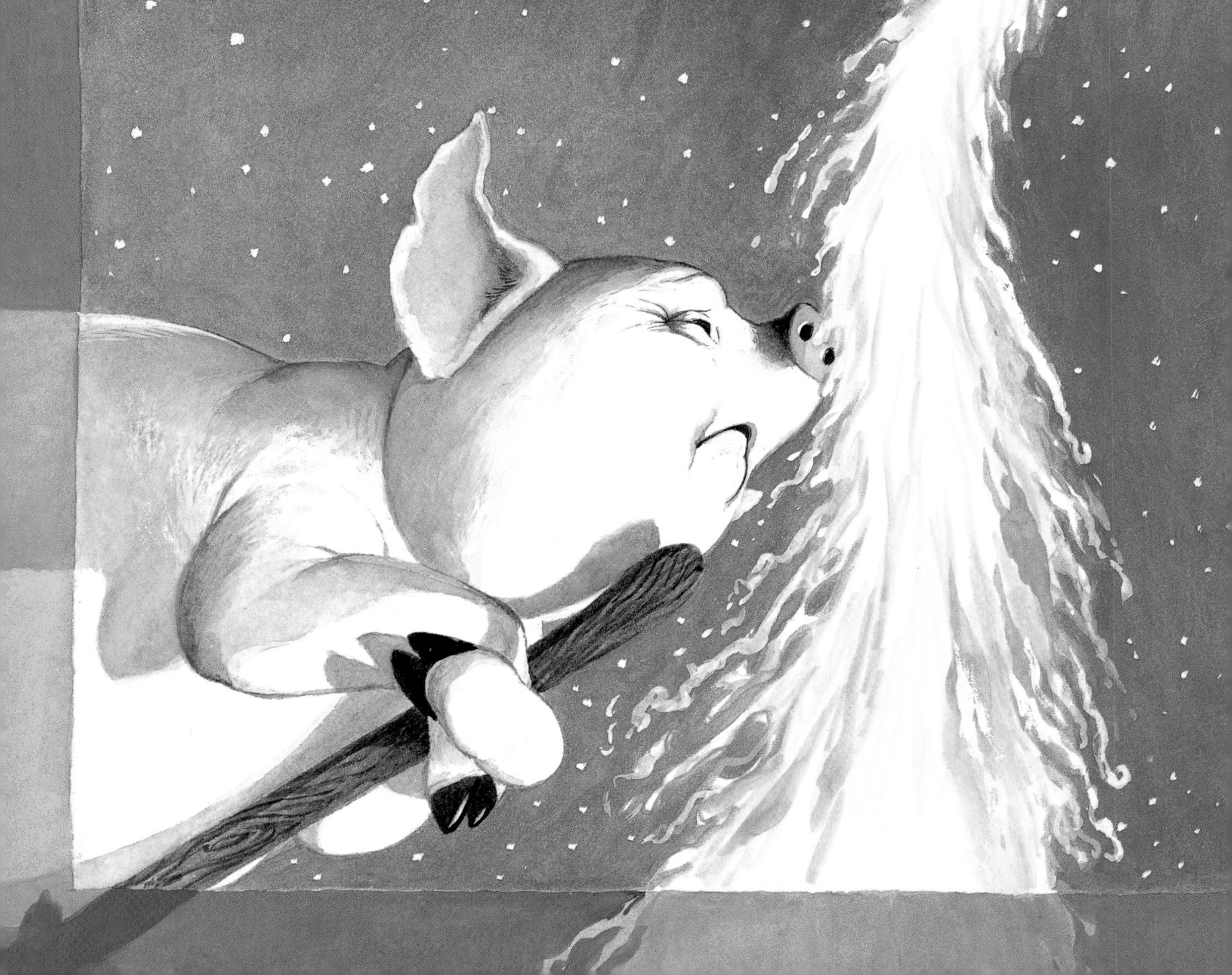

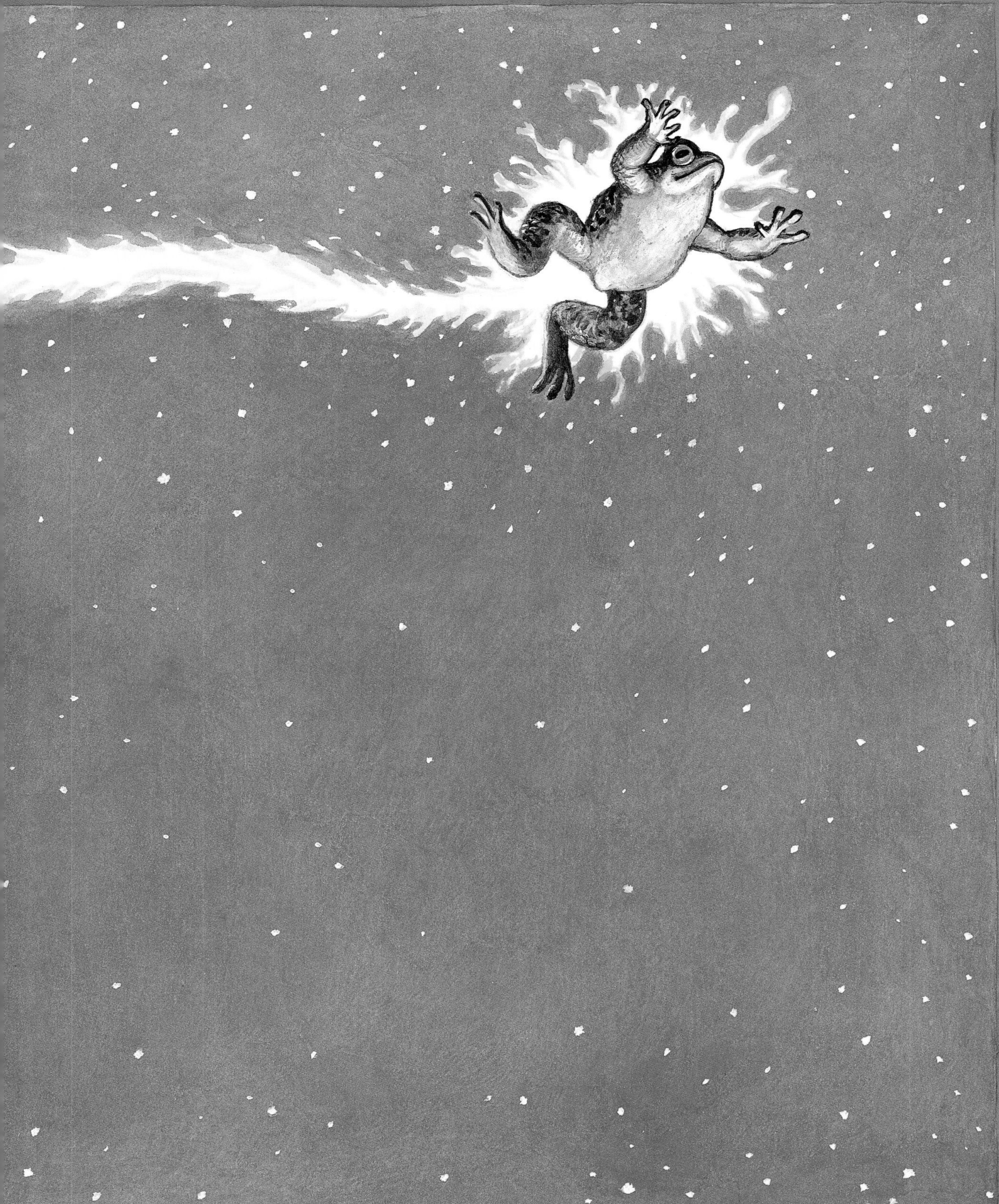

"Curses!" howled the witch, hopping up and down wrathfully.

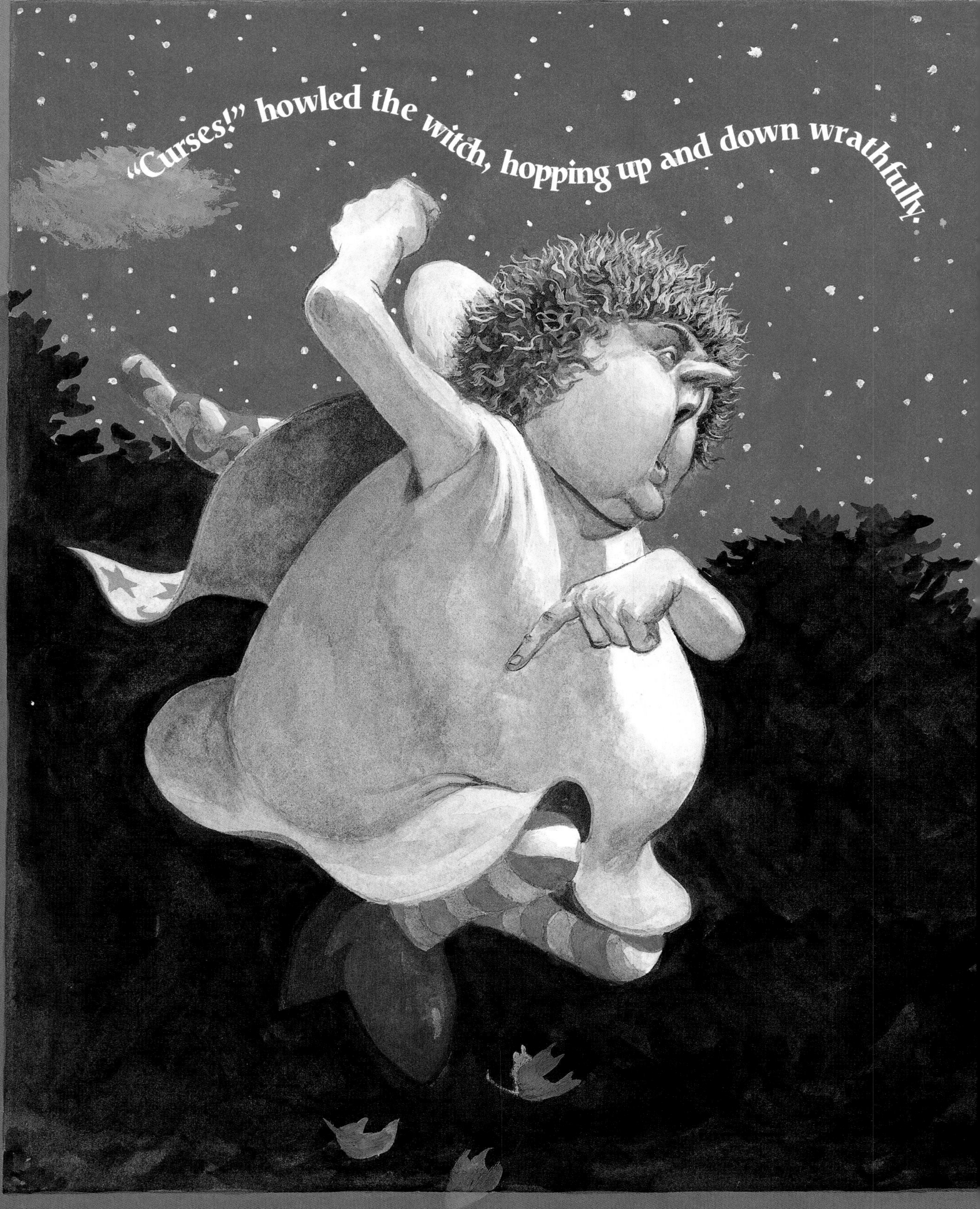

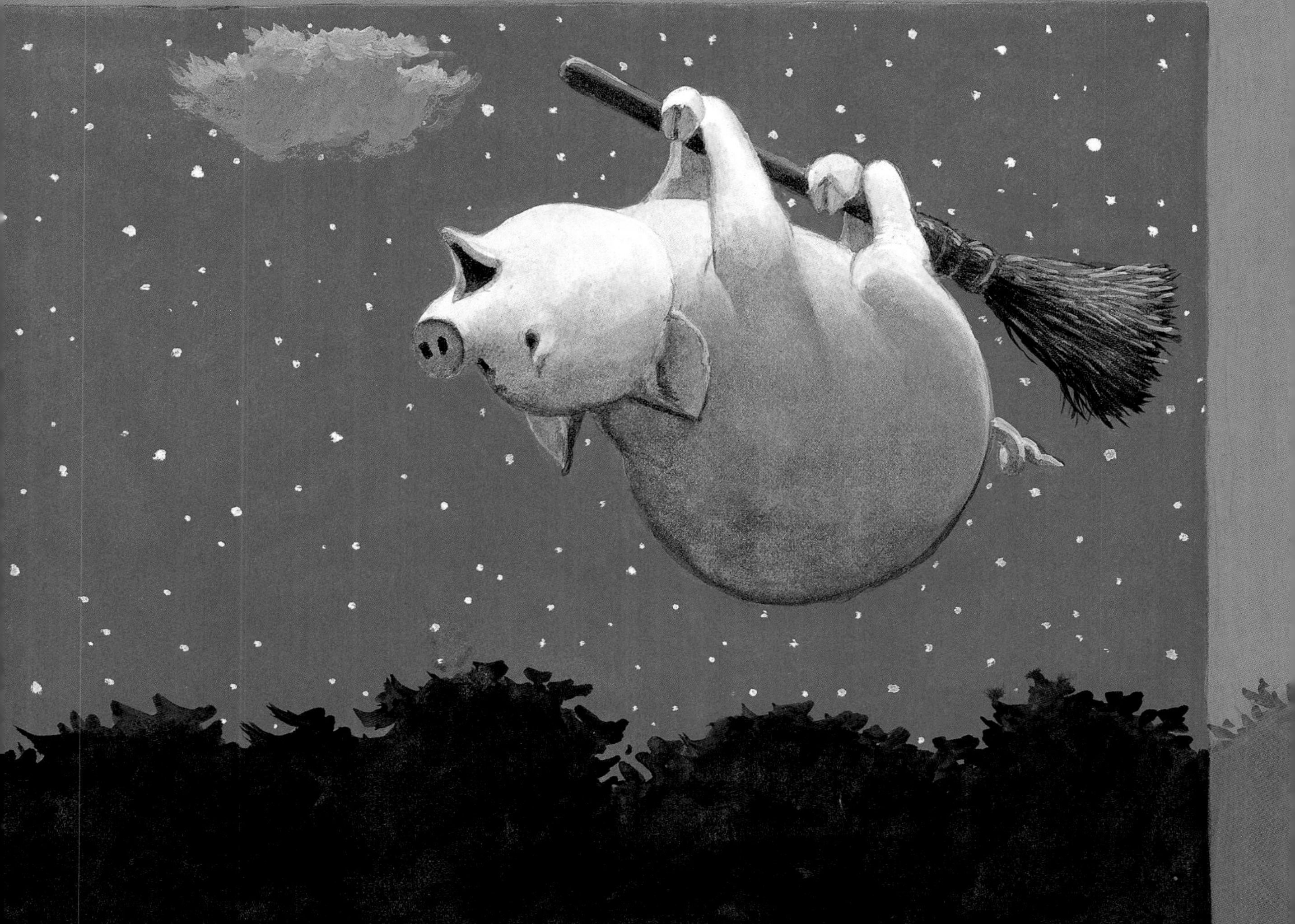

"Bring back my broom, or I will turn you into a . . . a . . . a . . . a bee!"

"I keep telling you," screamed Elwood from up in the air, "I don't know how to land!"

The witch was beside herself with rage. She threw up her arms, gritted her teeth, and launched her spell.

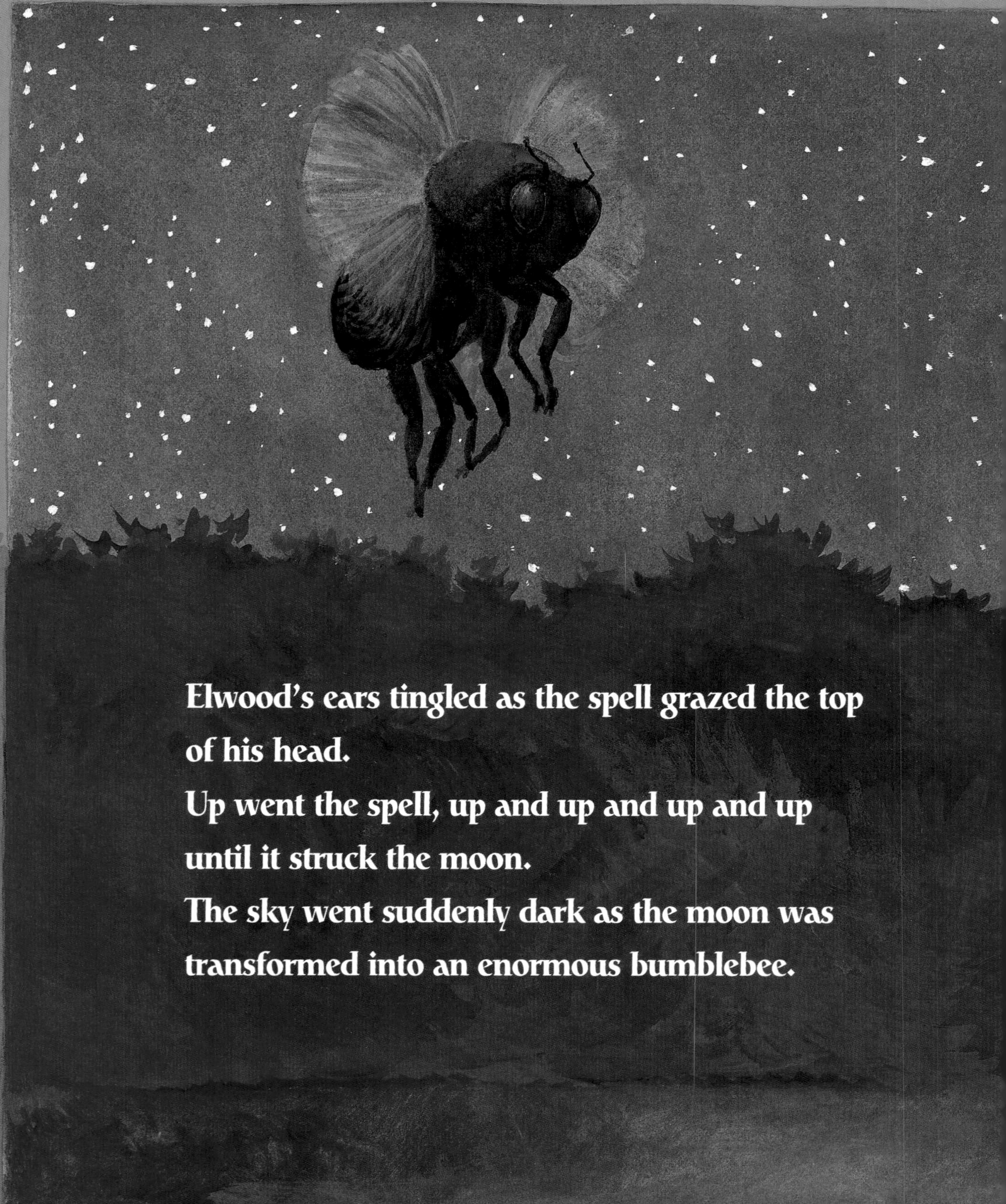

Elwood's ears tingled as the spell grazed the top of his head.

Up went the spell, up and up and up and up until it struck the moon.

The sky went suddenly dark as the moon was transformed into an enormous bumblebee.

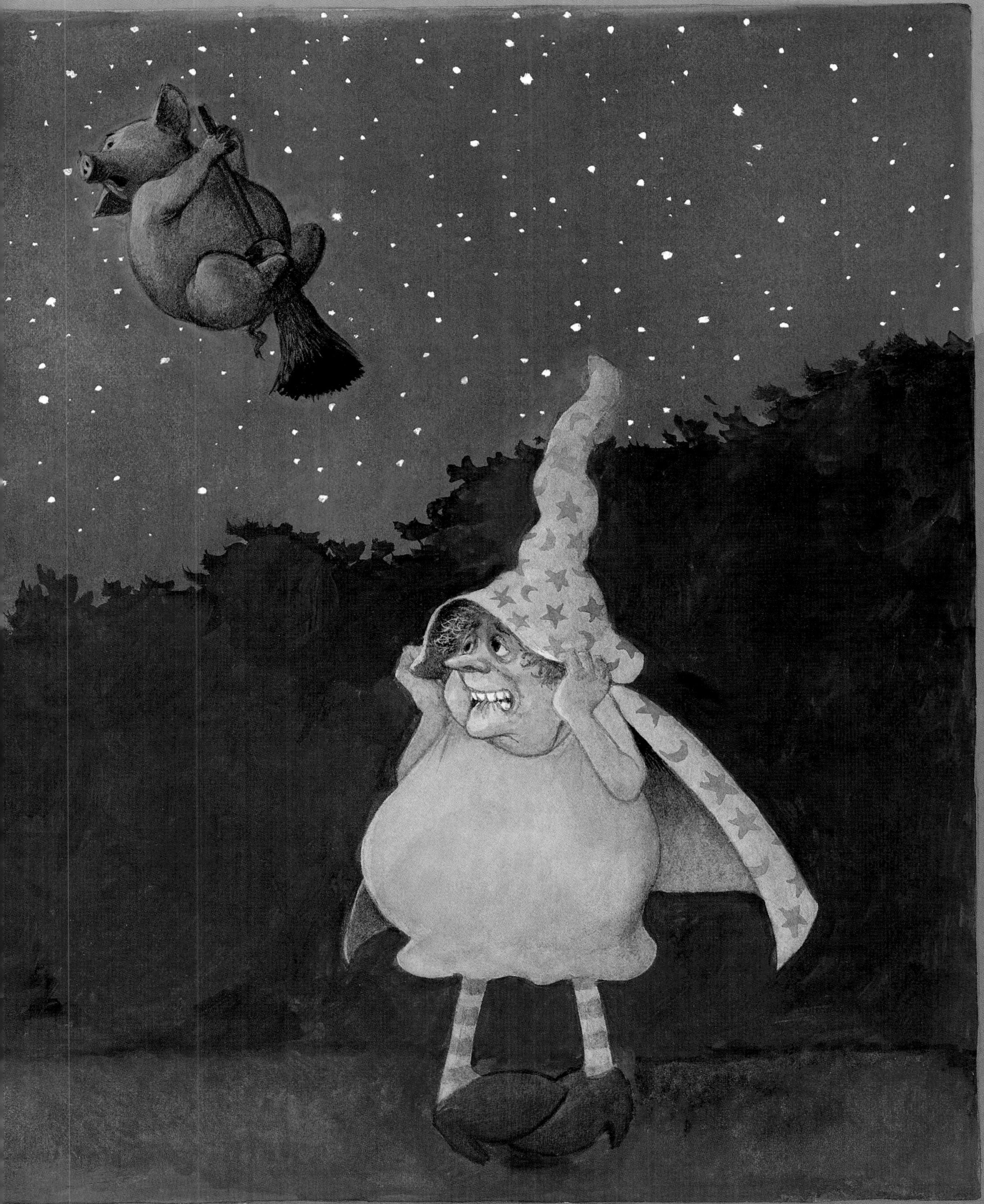

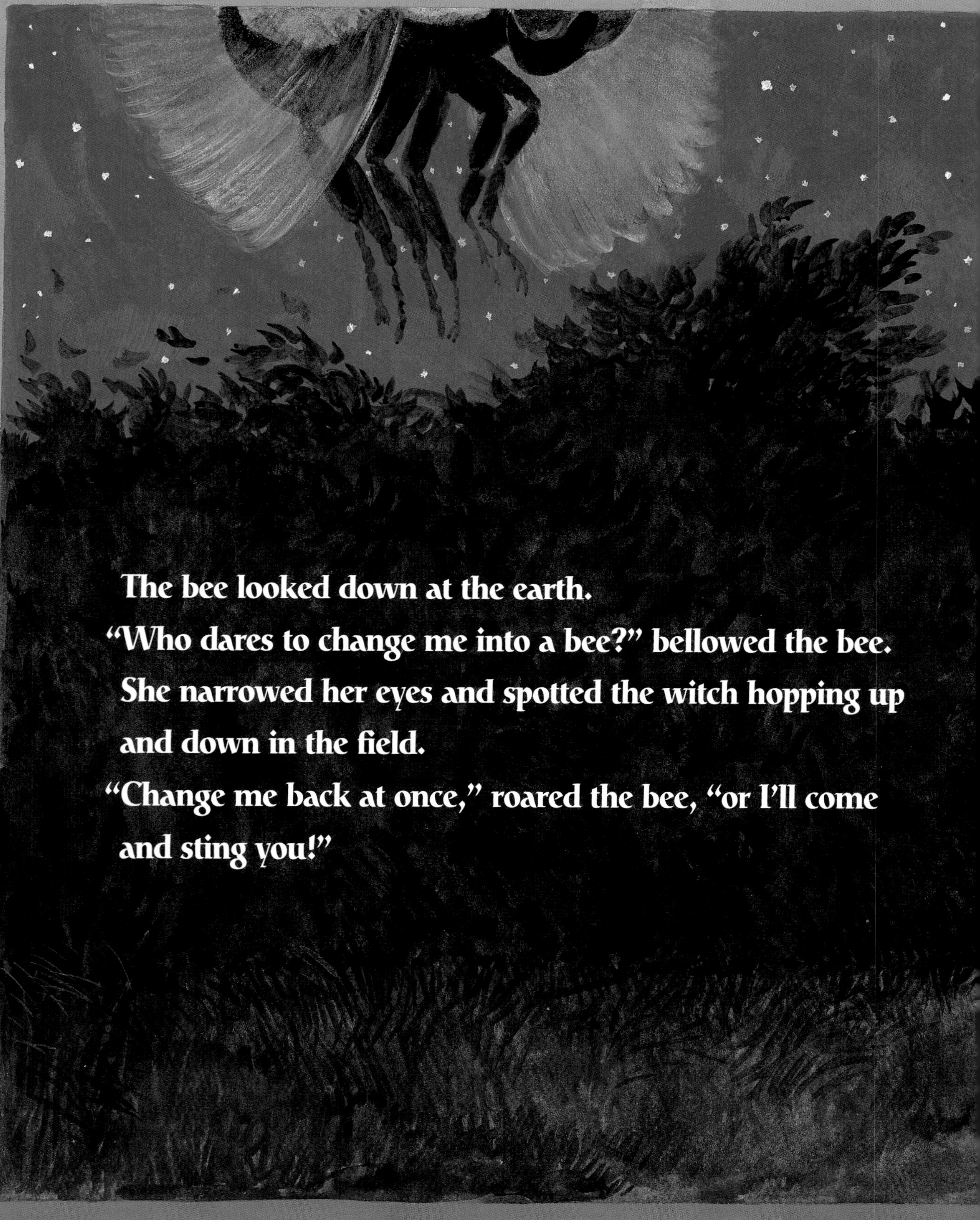

The bee looked down at the earth.

"Who dares to change me into a bee?" bellowed the bee.

She narrowed her eyes and spotted the witch hopping up and down in the field.

"Change me back at once," roared the bee, "or I'll come and sting you!"

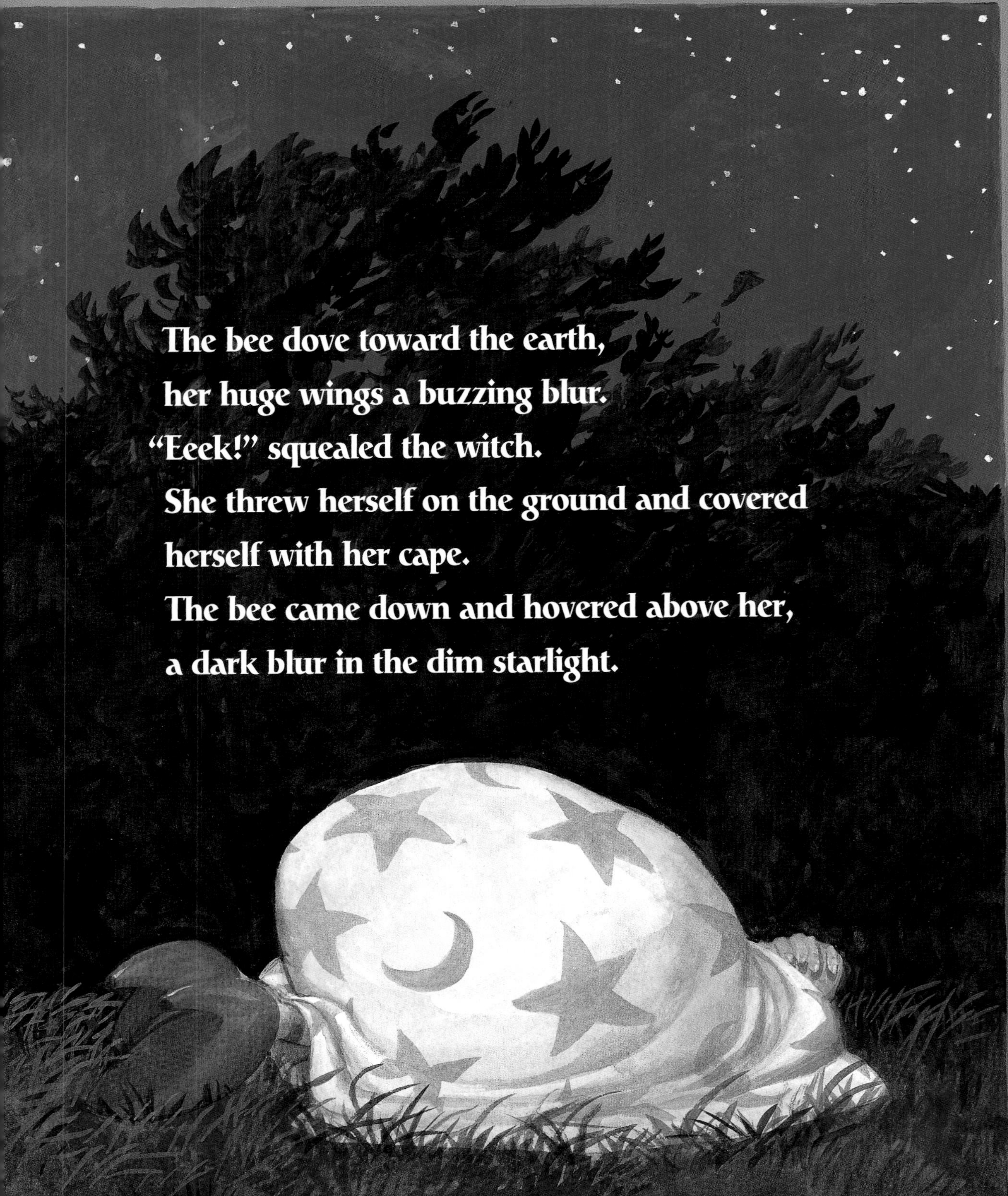

The bee dove toward the earth,
her huge wings a buzzing blur.
"Eeek!" squealed the witch.
She threw herself on the ground and covered
herself with her cape.
The bee came down and hovered above her,
a dark blur in the dim starlight.

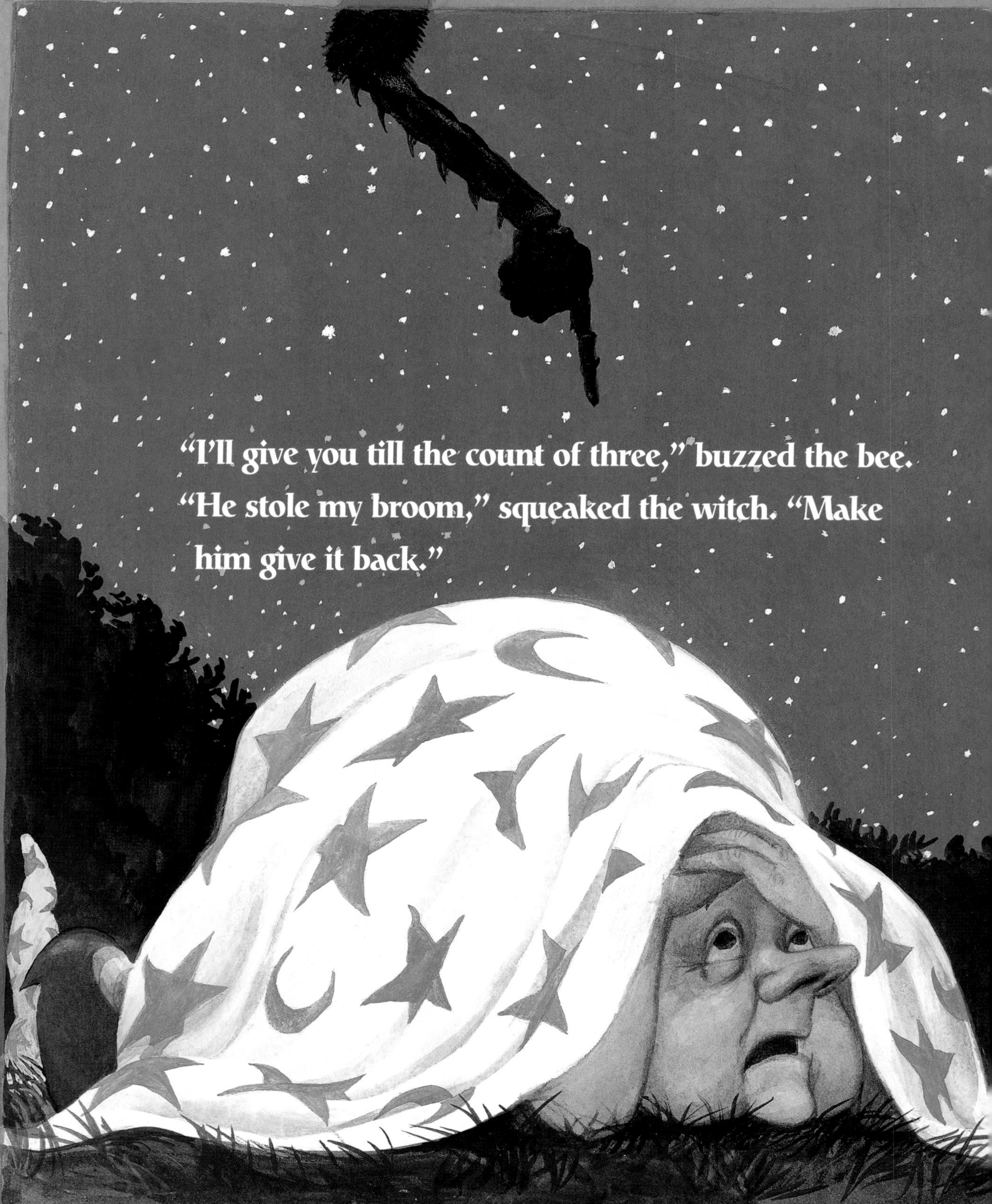

"I'll give you till the count of three," buzzed the bee.
"He stole my broom," squeaked the witch. "Make him give it back."

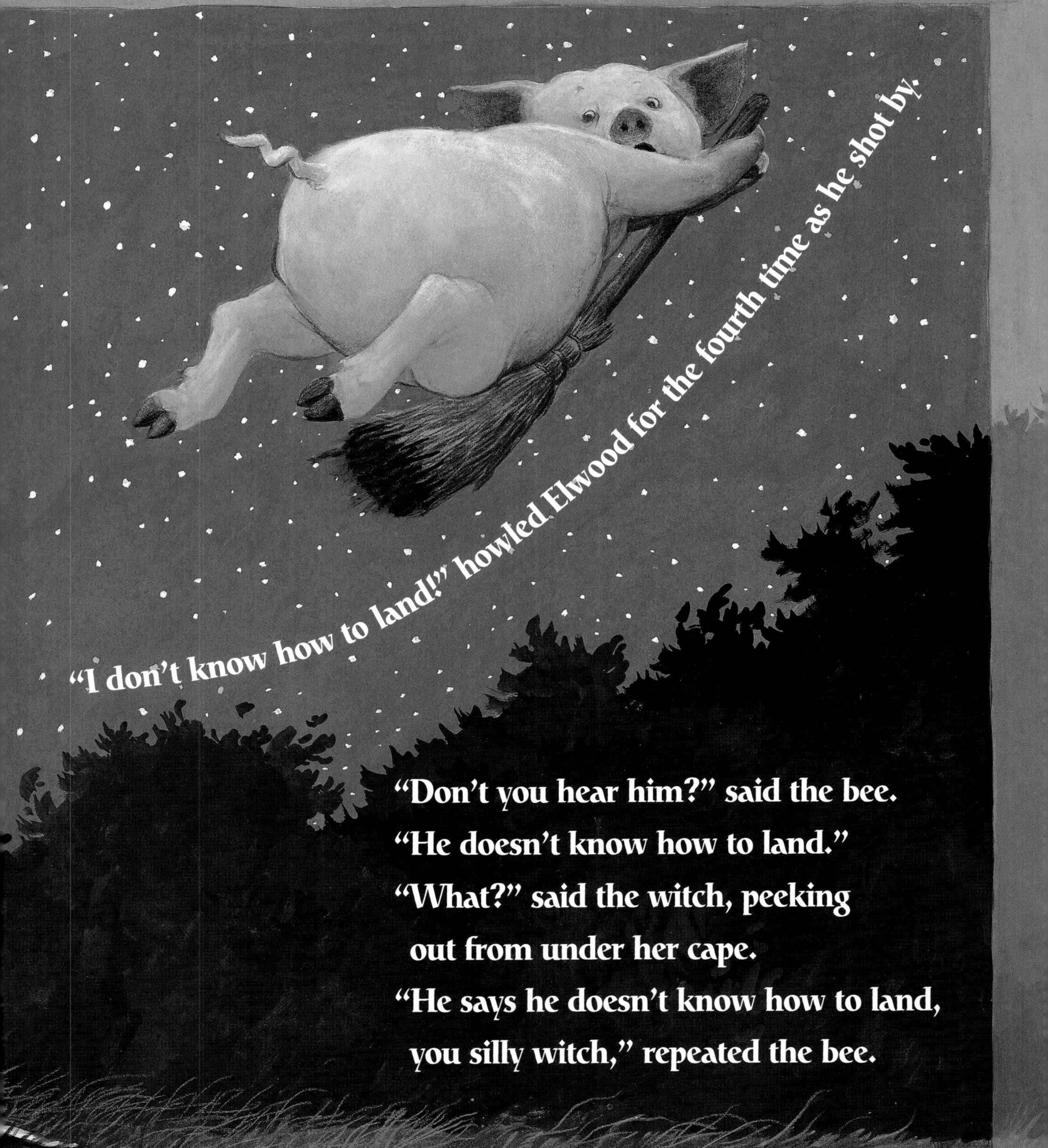

"I don't know how to land!" howled Elwood for the fourth time as he shot by.

"Don't you hear him?" said the bee.
"He doesn't know how to land."
"What?" said the witch, peeking
out from under her cape.
"He says he doesn't know how to land,
you silly witch," repeated the bee.

"Oh," said the witch. "It's just like any broom.
Push right to go left, pull up to go down."
Elwood pulled up on the end of the broomstick.
The broom headed downward.
Elwood pushed to the left and the broom
turned to the right.

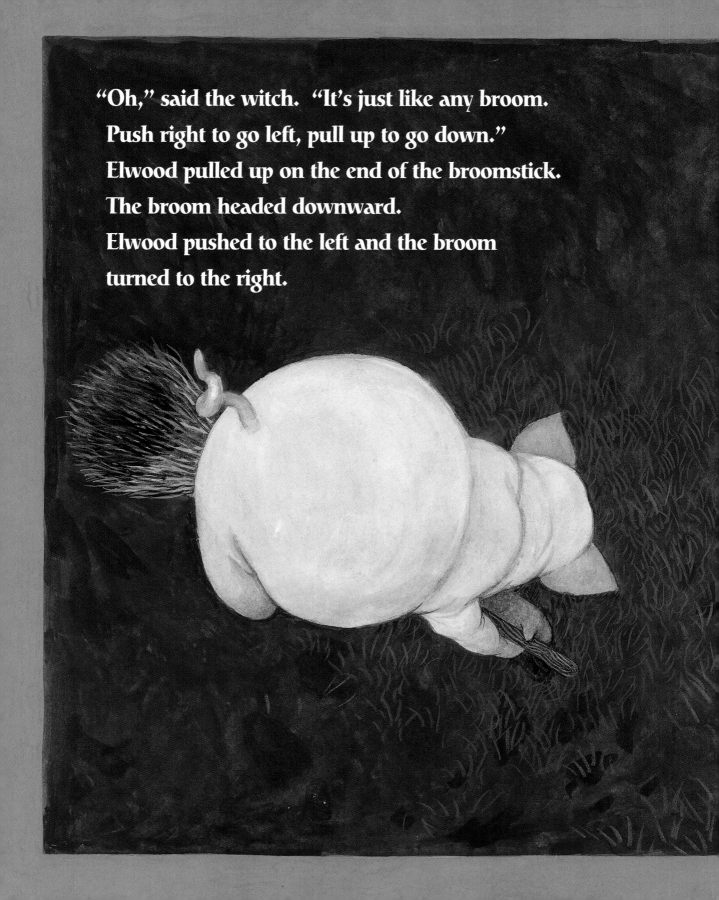

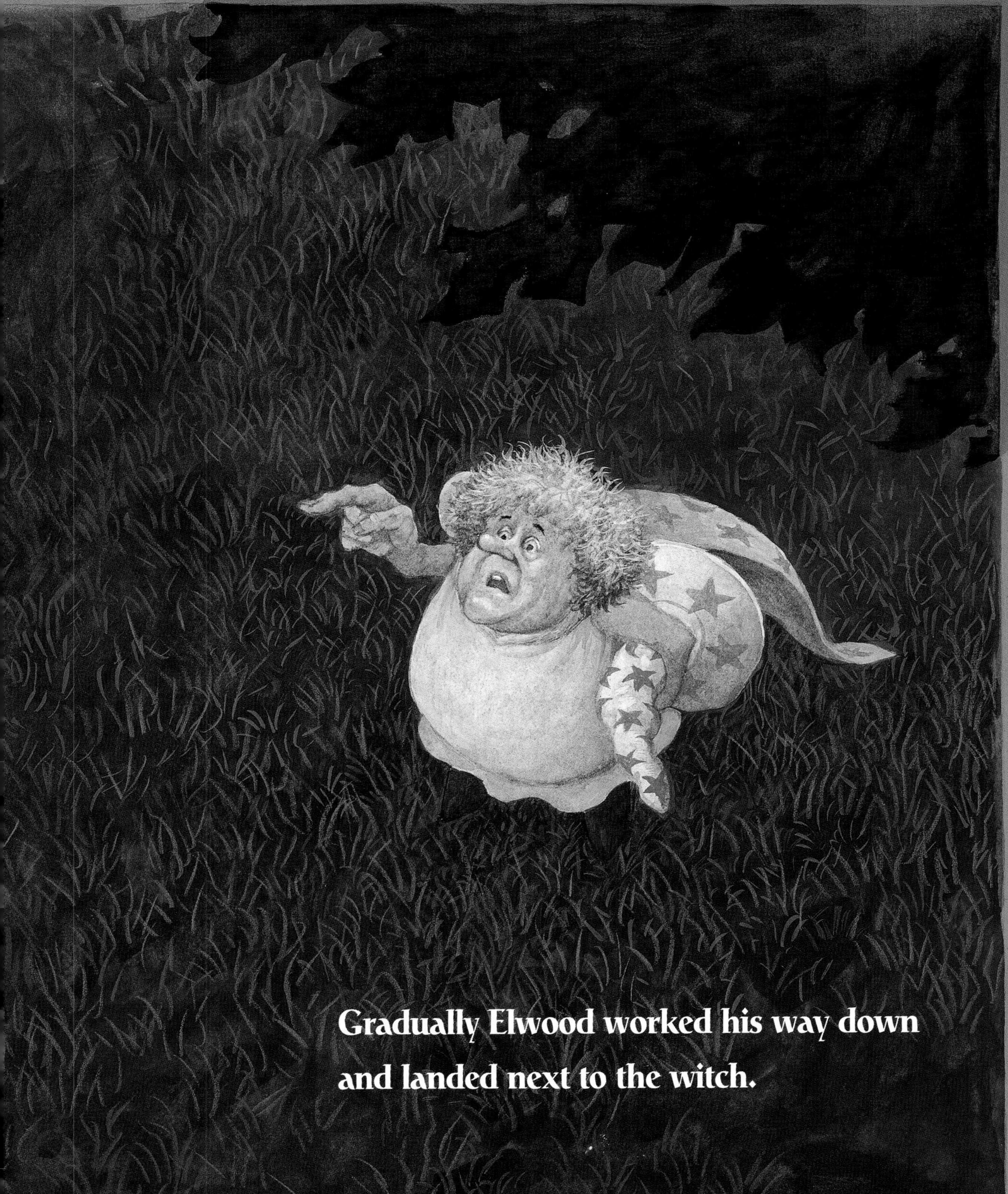

Gradually Elwood worked his way down
and landed next to the witch.

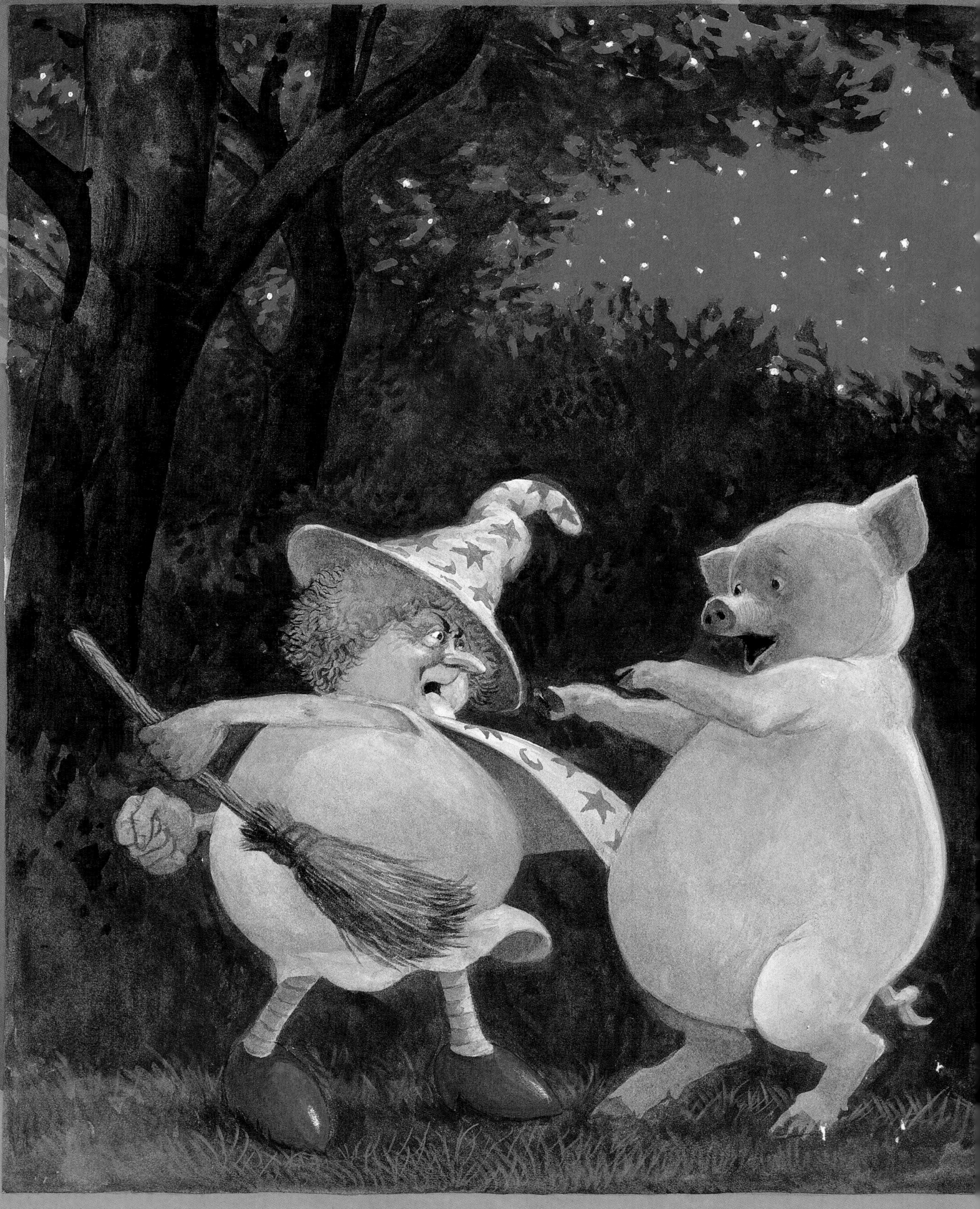

"Here's your broom," he said. "I certainly
   don't want it."
"Well, you can't have it!" snapped the witch,
   snatching it.
"Now change me back!" boomed the bee.
"And leave that pig alone," she added as she
   flew back into the sky. "I'll be watching."

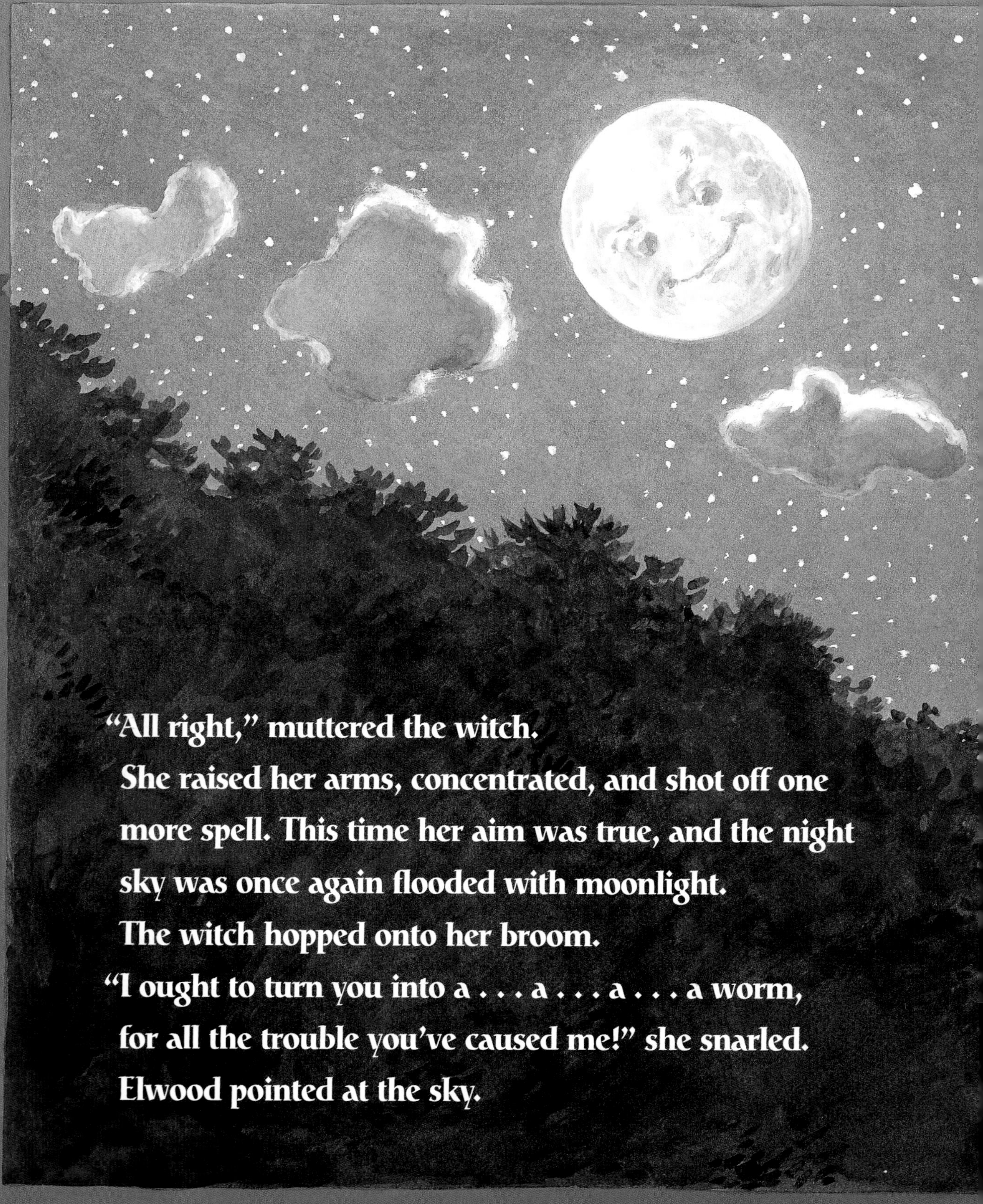

"All right," muttered the witch.

She raised her arms, concentrated, and shot off one more spell. This time her aim was true, and the night sky was once again flooded with moonlight.

The witch hopped onto her broom.

"I ought to turn you into a . . . a . . . a . . . a worm, for all the trouble you've caused me!" she snarled.

Elwood pointed at the sky.

"Remember, the moon's watching," he replied.
"Humph," muttered the witch, and she shot away.

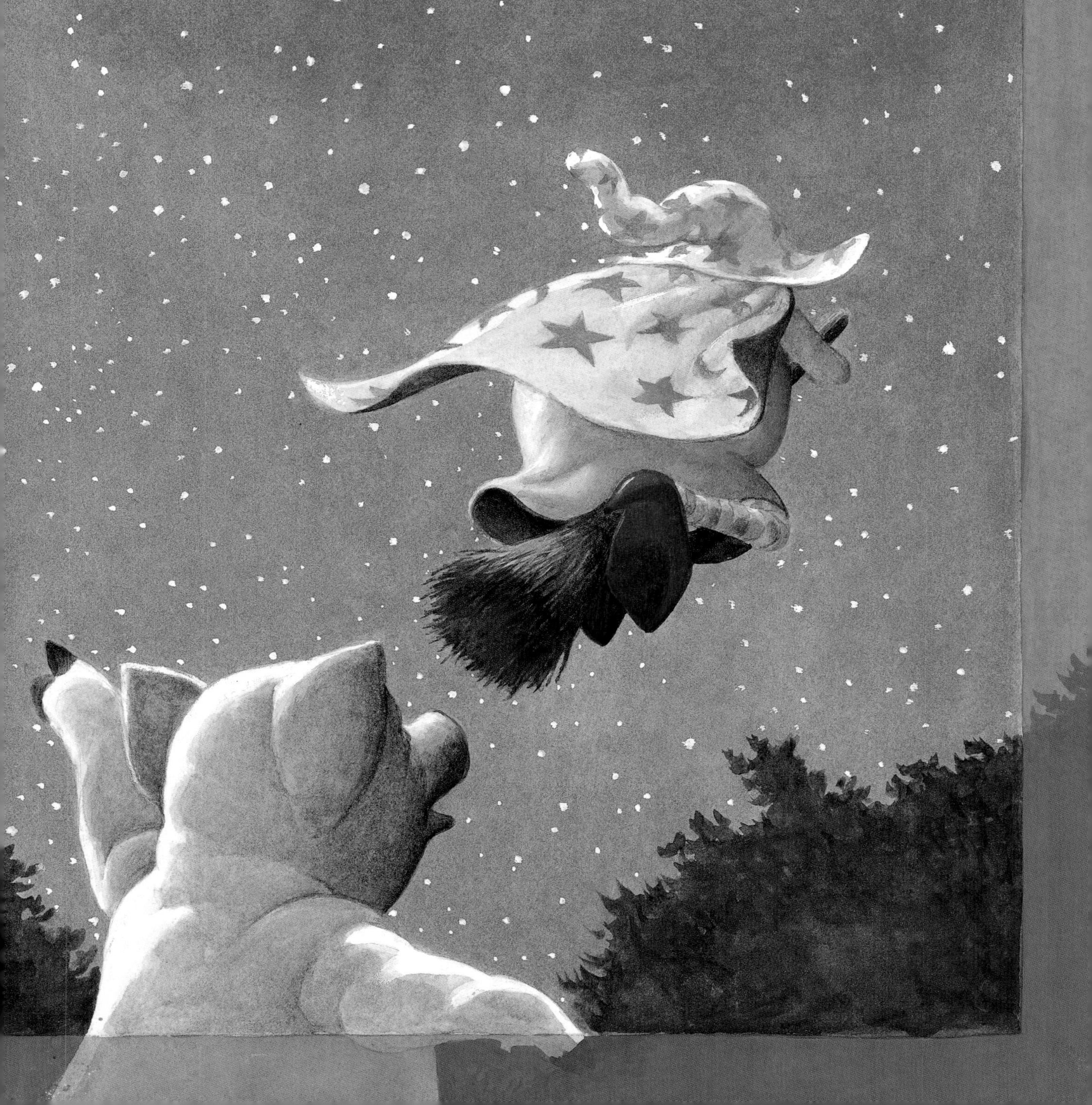

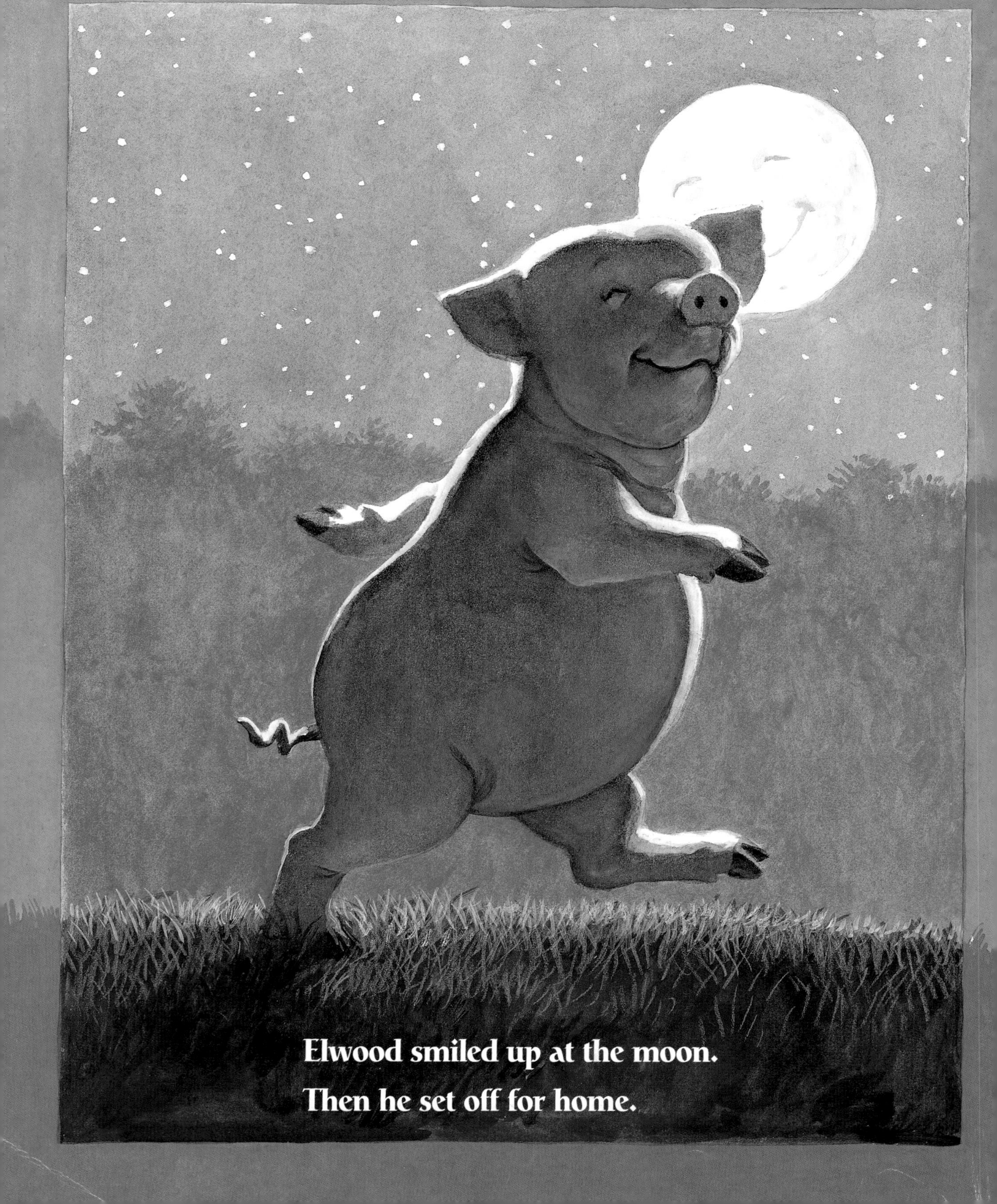

Elwood smiled up at the moon.
Then he set off for home.